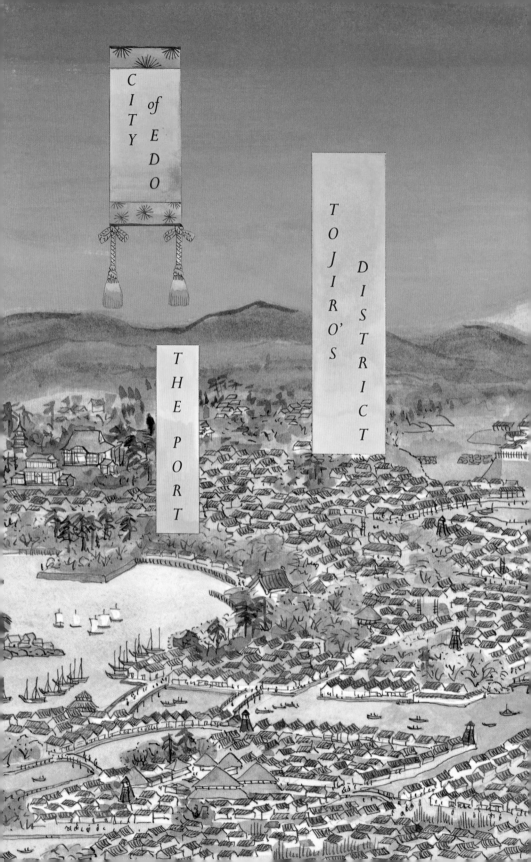

CITY of EDO

THE PORT

TOJIRO'S DISTRICT

MOUNT FUJI

CASTLE of the SHOGUN

The Old Man
Mad About
Drawing

FRANÇOIS PLACE

THE OLD MAN MAD ABOUT DRAWING

A Tale of Hokusai

translated from the French by
WILLIAM RODARMOR

DAVID R. GODINE · *Publisher*

BOSTON

First U.S. edition published in 2004 by
David R. Godine · *Publisher*
Post Office Box 450
Jaffrey, New Hampshire 03452
WWW.GODINE.COM

Originally published in French as *Le vieux fou de dessin*,
by Éditions Gallimard Jeunesse, Paris, in 1997.

Copyright © 2001 by Éditions Gallimard Jeunesse, Paris

Translation copyright © 2003 by William Rodarmor

Library of Congress Cataloging-in-Publication Data

Place, François
[Le vieux fou de dessin. English]
Old Man Mad About Drawing / by François Place;
translated from the French by William Rodarmor
p.   cm.
I. Rodarmor, William   II. Title

THIRD PRINTING, 2008
Printed in Italy

CONTENTS

FOR ANAÏS

Every morning, Tojiro took his basket of rice cakes and went out to make his deliveries. It was barely dawn and an occasional lantern feebly illuminated the streets. A few loaded boats slid along the canals and a few roosters crowed in the bottoms of the gardens, but the artisans' painted shops already echoed with the bright clanging of tools. The great city of Edo was waking up.

Tojiro sold his cakes to passersby, but also to the straw-hat seller, to the beautiful ladies of the tea-house, to the carpenter, the barrel maker, the potter, the blacksmith,

the barber, the dyer, and the public scribe, who always winked at him.

Sometimes he was lucky enough to sell one to a samurai proudly striding along with his two swords stuck in his belt. Tojiro would bow more seriously than usual when he took the money, trying to put on his face the impassive expression of a fierce warrior. Then he would straighten up and set off again, shouting his little street vendor's song at the top of his lungs.

The people of the neighborhood all knew him. He was a lively, cheerful boy, who chirped and hopped from store to store with the rumpled grace of a disheveled sparrow.

Tojiro had lost his parents and lived with his uncle and aunt. But life with his uncle was hard. When Tojiro finished his morning rounds, he would come back to fetch a second basket, and return home only when he had sold all of his cakes. Very often that was at nightfall.

In the summer it was a pleasant job. But in winter, when it snowed,

when it was freezing, when rain rattled in volleys on the city's roofs and the cold erased people's smiles, the boy trotting along under his thin rice-straw cape found the basket very heavy.

Just the same, Tojiro was proud to live in Edo, the capital of Japan, and to walk along its narrow streets bordered by so many wooden houses, stalls, temples, palaces, and gardens. He loved the animation of the reed-lined canals, the smell of the sea, and the distant silhouette of Mount Fuji. It was said that a million people lived in Edo. As you can imagine, you could run into all sorts of people there!

Among Tojiro's customers was a strange man, an old

grump who lived near a little canal that flowed into the Sumida River.

The man was very poor and ill-tempered, and wore shabby clothes. Yet he was often visited by high-class people, merchants from the elegant neighborhoods, or noblemen dressed in silk.

Under his bushy white eyebrows, the old gentleman's eyes gleamed like two brilliant black pieces of coal. Each time he saw the boy, he gave a little laugh like a cough and called to him in a mocking tone.

"So, sparrow, what fine things are you bringing me today?"

"Rice cakes, master," always answered the boy, who had never sold anything else.

"Rice cakes, eh? In that case give me one of your cakes, sparrow."

Tojiro wished the old man would stop calling him sparrow: He sold rice cakes to samurai – people ought to take him a little more seriously! But he took the coin in his hand and bowed, saying nothing. And the old man's laughter accompanied him when he turned on his heels to continue on his rounds.

A SCUFFLE NEAR
THE OLD BRIDGE

Eventually, Tojiro learned what this odd character did for a living: He was an artist. A great artist, said the people of the neighborhood. That was all Tojiro knew, except that the old man never stopped drawing. Oh well, it's a job like any other, the boy told himself — though he set the honor of being a samurai above all else — and it doesn't even make you rich. Be that as it may, a customer is a customer, and a rice cake sold is a rice cake sold, and the old gentleman's studio was on his route, not very far from the bridge across the canal that leads to the Sumida River.

He's an artist and that's all there is to it, thought Tojiro as he approached the painter's studio one day. As it happened, a crowd of people was blocking the road.

13

 People were pushing and shoving and chattering among themselves. One man, red with anger, was yelling and waving his fists under the face of the painter, who was standing very calmly at his garden gate.

"Crazy old man!" screamed the angry fellow.

Tojiro wasn't quite sure what to do. He was a little bit frightened, but he also very much wanted to get a little bit closer. Like all of Edo's inhabitants, Tojiro loved stories, and he walked through the city's streets as if he were in an open-air theater. Insults flew, a few blows were struck, people grabbed each other by the sleeve. But nothing calmed the angry man, who was becoming even more furious and waving his arms around like windmills. It took three husky fellows from the carpentry shop next door to subdue him and drag him out of the crowd, still screaming.

"Let me go! He's a crazy old man, I tell you!"

The argument ended as quickly as it began. The crowd scattered. Here and there, people stood gossiping about the event, laughing and nudging each other.

Impassive, the old painter greeted Tojiro as he had every other day. He was very calm and seemed to have already forgotten the incident.

"Ah, there you are, sparrow. What good things are you bringing me today?"

"Why did the gentleman call you a crazy old man?"

"Oh, it's nothing. It's just because one of my drawings didn't turn out."

"Don't you want to tell me? Do you think I'm too little?"

"No. I just gave you the answer."

15

"Then you're making fun of me," said Tojiro, sighing with disappointment.

"Uh, oh, our sparrow isn't in a good mood today. But I'm not making fun of you. I drew a shishi wrong."

"A shishi?"

"It's a sort of lion-dragon good-luck animal."

"Did the gentleman also want a lion-dragon?"

"I don't think so. This gentleman doesn't care about lions in general or about drawing in particular. Uh, oh, what's happening? Our sparrow isn't going to start crying, is he?"

"It's just that you're still making fun of me," answered Tojiro, balling his fists. "If this gentleman didn't have anything to do with your drawing, why did he call you a crazy old man?"

The painter gestured to the boy to come in. From a low table he took a sheet of white paper with a drawing, its ink still wet, of a roaring lion.

"See for yourself," he said. And Tojiro's eyes widened

as he looked at the most beautiful picture of a shishi he had seen in his life.

"But this drawing didn't turn out badly at all," he stammered. "It's even . . . magnificent! You're making fun of me again."

"Hmm. . . . Well, actually you may be right. The drawing isn't too bad," said the old man, comically leaning his head over the little boy's shoulder. "You know, I draw a shishi every morning so that the day is favorable for me. It's a good-luck drawing, if you like. Today's drawing didn't keep me from having trouble, as you could see. That's why I said it didn't turn out. Uh, oh, I see that in your sparrow's eye you're not too far from thinking me a crazy old man, too!"

Tojiro shifted his weight from one foot to the other, looking now at the drawing, now at the old man. A wide smile suddenly brightened his face.

"Ha, ha, ha!" said the old man. "What do you say to that, sparrow?"

And the two of them burst out laughing.

TOJIRO'S SHISHI

Next day, Tojiro could hardly wait to get to the old painter's house. This character greatly intrigued him.

As soon as he arrived, he asked to see the shishi the painter had drawn that day.

"Uh, oh, our sparrow is very inquisitive this morning," said the old man, showing him a drawing of a shishi scratching itself.

"It's magnificent, master. Just magnificent!"

"Well, in that case, it is yours. I am giving it to you."

Tojiro bowed as low as if he were bowing to a samurai.

二月
廿三

"Master, allow me to give you a rice cake in exchange."

"Thank you, little sparrow. I am sure it will be the best of rice cakes," said the old man, bowing very ceremoniously in turn.

Tojiro bowed three times more and withdrew, pressing the rolled-up drawing to his chest. Then he resumed his rounds with his heart pounding, full of joy at having received such a prestigious gift.

But when he came back the next day, he barely dared enter the house. His face was pale and his right eye sported an ugly blue bruise.

Without a word, he handed the drawing to the old painter.

"It seems that my drawing didn't bring you luck, sparrow. Have you displeased your parents?" asked the old man.

"My uncle scolded me. He told me to give it back to you and to make you pay for yesterday's rice cake."

"Your uncle gets angry quickly. I think he's a little like my grandson."

"You have a grandson?"

"Of course. He's the one you saw leaving here two days ago, calling me a crazy old man. Do you remember?"

"Now you're making fun of me again. That man was much too old to be your grandson."

"Tell me, how old are you?"

"Nine years old, master."

"Well, I will soon be ten times as old as you. So you see, I can have a grandson old enough to be your father. Which doesn't keep him from being a good-for-nothing who spends all his time drinking and running up debts."

That last sentence finished cheering Tojiro up. He raised his little finger and gravely recited: "'At the first cup, the man drinks the sake; at the second cup, the sake drinks the sake; at the third cup, the sake drinks the man.' That's what my uncle often says."

"I see that you are learning well, but in my opinion your uncle should stop after the first cup. A gift is a gift, so keep the drawing. I'll pay you for yesterday's cake and today's, and we'll be even. Tell me, little sparrow. Do you know how to read?"

"No," the child answered, blushing.

"It so happens that I need an assistant, a sharp boy like you to go fetch my inks and my paper, and to bring my drawings to the engraving studio. I think you would be perfect for the job, but you must learn to read and write. What do you say? If my proposal interests you, I'll go speak to your uncle."

"In that case your drawing will really have brought me luck, master," answered Tojiro with a big smile, winking his black eye.

Within a few days, an agreement was reached with Tojiro's uncle. The boy would work for the painter in the morning, and in exchange the old man would take charge of his education and furnish him all the material he needed to learn to read and write: books, paper, and brushes.

The old painter called himself Hokusai.

His house had hundreds of books and prints, several low tables crowded with jars of ink sticks and powdered colors, partly finished drawings, a teapot, lacquer boxes, and carved black wood blocks.

"The first thing I expect of you, sparrow, is to never straighten up my studio. The second is to always be curious and to open your eyes and ears wide. The third is to never bother me while I'm working.

洲之助

あり衣

よば七

夢を占して
鮮衣
その方
洲之助と
数を

Today, all you have to do is look at these books. They should appeal to you, since you like samurai."

Tojiro sat down in a corner of the studio with the first book he found. He opened a page at random and immediately gave a cry of horror. He had never seen such a frightening picture!

Then he turned another page, and soon each of the illustrations produced an "Oh!" of surprise or admiration. They showed groups of horsemen, warriors caught in snowstorms, monstrous battles between men and giants, and apparitions of spirits and ghosts. Each character seemed so alive that the young boy sometimes imagined himself entering into the picture.

"This old painter is a magician," Tojiro said to himself. "What a pity that I can't read the story. If he would agree to lend me one of these books, maybe the public scribe would read it to me."

At the end of the morning the young boy was still absorbed by the images. The old man had to shake him by the shoulder to draw him from his contemplation.

"Master, are you really the one who did the drawings in this book?"

"Of course, sparrow, and many more besides."

"You're a magician! I've never seen anything so beautiful!"

"Thank you," answered the old man. "I am happy to have given you such joy. Your compliments go straight to my heart.

"Today is your first day, so I am going to invite you to share a meal with me. There is a little tofu restaurant right at the end of the street. I hope that my books haven't spoiled your appetite."

"To the contrary, master. I could eat a whole shishi."

"Have you already forgotten that it's my good-luck animal?" said the old painter, bringing his eyebrows together into a dramatic frown.

"Forgive me, master," said Tojiro, suddenly abashed.

"Let's go," said the old painter with a burst of laughter. "I'm as hungry as a lion as well!"

During lunch, Tojiro thought back to the books whose pictures he had so admired. One question greatly intrigued him. The old man's library had several copies of

certain books. How did the old painter go about illustrating the same book several times over?

Tojiro paused.

"Master, is it true that you can find ten or fifteen copies of the same work in a bookstore?"

"Yes, and even many more than that."

"Does this mean that you do the same drawings over

again, as many times as there are books? Do you have to do an illustration ten times in a row? A hundred times?"

"Come now, of course not. A lifetime wouldn't be long enough. In books, my illustrations are printed. Reproduced, if you prefer."

"I understand," said Tojiro, with some disappointment. "Someone copies them for you."

29

"Not quite, sparrow. To print a picture you first have to engrave it."

"That's complicated."

"Only for a sparrow brain! Tomorrow you will go with me to a printer, and you will learn more."

C
H
A
P
T
E
R

5

THE WOODBLOCK
ENGRAVING STUDIO

When I was your age, I was a clerk in a large bookstore. But I did too many foolish things, and had to leave fairly quickly, so I became an apprentice in the studio of a woodblock carver. And gradually I learned the art of woodblock engraving."

"Woodblock engraving?"

"It sometimes happens that several art lovers want the same copy of an artist's work. As you can imagine, he isn't going to draw it hundreds of times. So he relies on people in other trades: the publisher, the engraver, and the printer. The artist gives the drawing to an engraver, who copies it in relief on a block of wood. The printer inks this carved block, lays a sheet of paper on it, and presses down on it: in this way the drawing is 'reproduced.' It's then called a print. Finally the publisher is the person who brings buyers and artists together. He picks the drawings, pays the engravers and printers, and sells the books or prints that come out of his studio. For my part, since I was very gifted, my master quickly suggested that I start creating my own designs. I became one of the best artists in the studio.

"We've arrived, sparrow. Come on, let's go in."

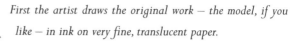

First the artist draws the original work — the model, if you like — in ink on very fine, translucent paper.

The engraver glues the drawing onto a block of carefully polished cherry wood, with the drawn side against the wood.

The model now appears backwards.

The engraver cuts away the wood around each line, so the entire drawing gradually emerges in relief.

For this work the engraver uses a mallet, knives, gouges, and wood chisels, which he must sharpen frequently.

The carved wood block is given to the printer, who carefully inks the block's surface, coating all of the lines and surfaces left in relief by the engraver.

The printer then lays a damp sheet of paper on the block and firmly rubs the surface of the paper with a baren.

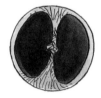

A baren is a lacquered disk wrapped in bamboo leaves.

The printer carefully lifts off the sheet of paper. . .

The print made on the sheet is absolutely identical to the artist's model. To produce another print, you need only ink the block again and press another sheet on it, and so forth, as many times as you want copies. When a print is in more than one color, you use a different carved block for each color.

35

In the studio, men were working. One was dampening sheets of paper with a broad brush. Another was sharpening tools on a grindstone set above a bucket of water. Two engravers were bent over their tables carving rectangular blocks of wood. The air was filled with a pleasant smell of ink, wood shavings, and paper. The only sound to be heard was the rubbing of brushes and the regular blows of a mallet on a chisel.

Tojiro was so impressed, he forgot to bow to the printer who welcomed them.

"Open your eyes and ears wide," said the old painter. "Here is your first lesson in woodblock engraving."

"You really have to do all that to print a picture? What a lot of work!" exclaimed Tojiro. "I would never be able to do that."

"That's the sort of thing one should never say at your age, sparrow. You know, even I am still learning. Yet I'm much older than you."

"Master, is this the way your books are printed?" said the child, suddenly dumbfounded.

"Of course, sparrow. That's how the different pages

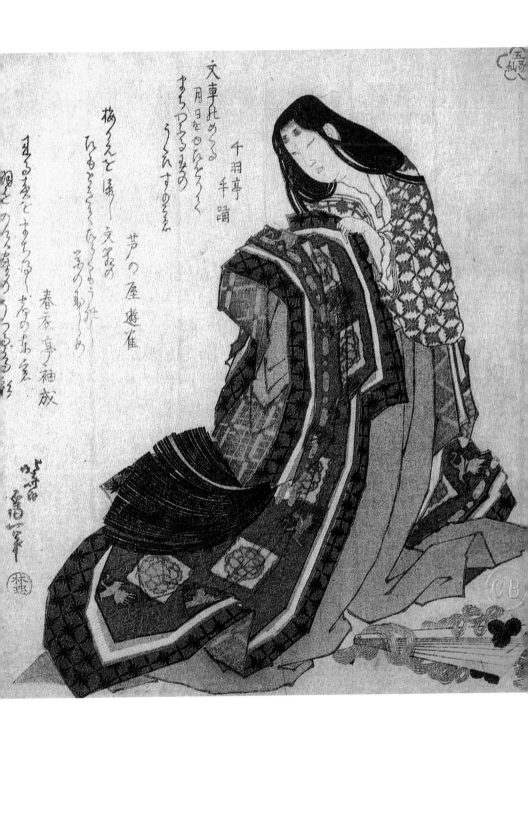

of a book are printed. They are then bound together with stitching. Woodblock printing lets you reproduce many other things as well: posters, suites of prints on a single subject, calendars, paper fans, surimono. . . ."

"What are surimono?"

"Those are extremely expensive prints, with many colors. It sometimes takes fifteen passes to print them. Some are even printed with gold, silver, or mica, a very shiny powdered mineral. To show the texture of cloth, the shape of a cloud, or the boiling foam of a torrent, embossing is sometimes used. That's a technique of making an impression without using any color; it creates shapes on the paper's surface."

While he answered Tojiro's questions, the old painter

was advising the engravers, here complaining about one man's poor carving of a block, there suggesting color corrections to another, or modifying a third's drawing. Nothing escaped Hokusai's sharp eye. He carefully examined each proof, worrying about the thickness and the densities of the inks.

"Light ink should be like a shellfish broth," he repeated, "and dark ink should have the consistency of pea soup."

Tojiro was very surprised to see how respectfully the people heeded his advice.

"This crazy old man may not be so crazy after all," the child said to himself.

A WILD CHILDHOOD

On the way home, Tojiro peppered his aged master with questions. As they walked and talked, they were suddenly stopped by a crowd gathered around a poster. It announced a sumo tournament: a wrestling match between those huge men who weighed more than two hundred pounds. This sort of event always sparked a lot of public interest, and everyone in the street was talking about it, praising the qualities of his favorite champion.

"Master, were you the one who drew this poster?"

"You disappoint me, sparrow. Look a little more closely. Can't you see it's the work of a beginner? Don't you think it's a little too clumsy for an old painter like me?"

40

"I thought that you did all of the drawings in Edo," answered Tojiro, sulking.

"Up to now, I have done more than thirty thousand drawings, but that's nothing compared to everything that's published in a great city like Edo."

"But weren't you ever clumsy?"

"Of course I was. But I learned very quickly, and I have no doubt that you will follow my path in turn. I was very wild. After my apprenticeship in engraving, I entered the studio of a famous master painter and engraver, Katsukawa Shunsho. I was eighteen then, it was in 1778. The studio was located near the pleasure quarter, very close to a Kabuki theater.

"We produced the posters that announced the performances. The great fashion was to paint the portraits of the most famous actors. We had many customers, and they all wanted a picture of their favorite actor. Very few left without buying a print! Others asked for pictures of geishas, the beautiful courtesans who served in the tea-houses. I worked a great deal and I met a lot of people.

"At the Kabuki theater, the

greatest actors sometimes did me the honor of inviting me into their dressing rooms. I drew them while they were putting on their makeup or rehearsing their lines. You should have seen them pose when they knew that they would appear on a poster! In the end I wound up knowing all the sets and costumes, and I practically knew the repertoire by heart: *The Story of the Forty-Seven Ronin*, *Yoshitsune and the Thousand Cherry Trees*, and *The Story of a Bonze and a Courtesan Who Became Bandits*.

"Many times, when I was carving a block in the studio, I could hear the

applause from the other side of the street as the audience greeted the appearance of an actor on the Flowered Path, the walkway that allows an actor to cross above the crowd to the stage.

"In the evening I would join my companions in a teahouse on the banks of the Sumida River.

"In the springtime, in the season of flowers, we would sometimes even rent a boat to go for a cruise in the moonlight. At that time of year the river is covered with thousands of boats out for a sail, lit by lanterns, and the banks are covered with stalls and little restaurants.

"The air was filled with songs and laughter. It was an enchanting spectacle.

"Even then, I couldn't help but bring along a few bound sheets of paper and some ink. There were so many surprising, poetic, or comical things to see: the pale moon brushed by the branches of a cherry tree, or a family of ducks suddenly disturbed by some poor devil drunk on sake falling into the water.

"The next day at dawn, after a very short night, I would return to the studio.

"As I said, it was a lot of work and a lot of fun.

Those of us who were painters, poets, writers, engravers, and actors, formed a separate world: We were the representatives of 'the floating world,' of everything that lived and moved in the city. At that time I also began to illustrate my first books. Oh, they were only cheap 'yellow-

cover' books — popular literature — but it was work I really liked. Every day brought its share of surprises. You'll see: If you acquire a taste for drawing, you won't be able to do without it, just like me. But I see that we have arrived. . . . So I'll see you tomorrow, sparrow!"

CHAPTER 7

The next day when he got to the painter's, Tojiro found two palanquins in the middle of the passageway. The waiting bearers were casually smoking their pipes. "That's interesting," thought the child, "the master has visitors." He had barely crossed the threshold of the garden when the old man grabbed him by the arm.

"Come on, let's get going, Tojiro! We're going to be late!"

"Where are we going?"

"It's a surprise. Come on, get moving. Climb into your palanquin."

It was the first time that Tojiro had used this means of transportation. Actually, it was rare to see children carried in palanquins this way, but the old man was an original who didn't care about habits and proprieties. Then they were off, somewhat jostled by the bearers' brisk trot.

It made Tojiro giggle. Using other people's feet for walking, what a funny idea! They crossed the fish market and then plunged into the labyrinth of streets and alleys, crossing a good twenty of those little arched bridges above the canals. In this way, going through neighborhood after neighborhood, they reached the grounds of a great temple, where they stopped.

 While the painter paid the bearers, who were catching their breath and wiping their brows after the effort of the long trip, the boy looked around.

A large crowd was pressing toward a huge gateway framed by scaffolding, on which barrels of sake carefully wrapped in rice paper were stacked.

Tojiro couldn't believe his eyes: He was in the courtyard of the Eko-in Temple, the famous temple where sumo contests were held! The old painter led him to the tiers, which were already crowded. Above their heads banners flapped in the wind.

49

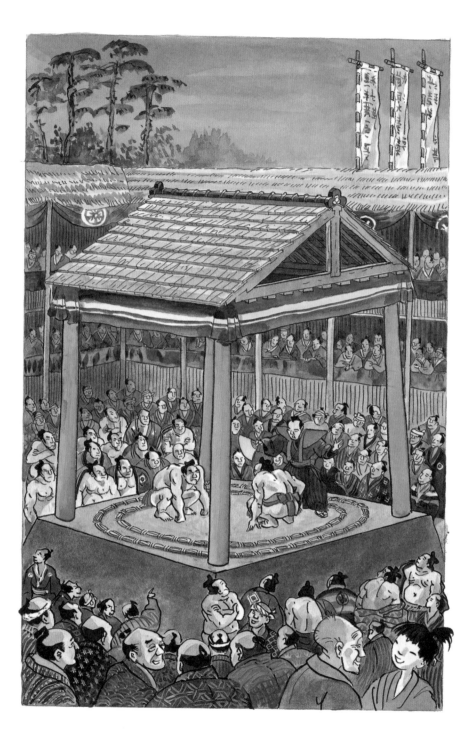

On a stage of pounded earth two great ropes of woven rice straw were laid in a perfect circle.

Suddenly, the sound of cedar-wood clappers rang out,

cutting through the hubbub. This signaled the entrance of the wrestlers. They walked in two lines, one to the east and one to the west, done up in their show loincloths and

aprons, and gravely saluted the crowd. Thunderous applause accompanied their procession.

The men were colossal. Tojiro thought them so big and so strong that they seemed to belong more to the world of gods than of men. They rolled their heads from left to right while shrugging their muscular shoulders.

Two of them, preceded by their trainers, climbed to the stage. The umpire spread his fan.

The wrestlers rinsed their mouths and threw salt on the ground. They clapped their hands, thrust to the side first

their right leg, then their left, and finally crouched opposite each other like two enormous frogs.

At the umpire's signal they threw themselves at each other, slapping their opponent with all their might. Roaring, they grabbed each other's belts and tried various holds. The audience stomped, cheered, and screamed at each attempt, and when silence fell you could hear the fighters' hoarse panting and the cracking of joints as their hands gripped in a new hold.

Suddenly, a single shout rose from the crowd. Quickly pivoting his hip, one of the wrestlers tipped his adversary over and threw him out of the circle like a ball of rice.

The winner raised his arms, as heavy and massive as two enormous clubs. He was answered by terrific applause. Already, two other adversaries were in the middle of the circle, ready to confront each other.

The old master observed Tojiro on the sly. The child's eyes had never shone so brightly.

TOJIRO'S DREAMS

That night Tojiro had trouble sleeping. As he tossed and turned in his sleep, the door to his room slid open and two bandits entered the room. He recognized them as sumo wrestlers. He jumped up and drove them off thanks to the master's paint-brushes.

"Get back, you clumsy oafs! Get back, or I'll draw you backwards!"

No sooner had that bad dream disappeared than a band of samurai straight out of a book galloped through the painter's studio.

The master didn't seem to pay

them much attention.
He was far too busy painting
ghosts, using five paintbrushes, one in
his mouth and one in each hand and foot.

"Go home to where you belong," the old man
abruptly hissed between his teeth. "Clear off! Get out of
here, or I'll call my grandson!"

"Crazy old man," the samurai answered.
"We're going to make you drink your ink
and then we're going to cut you to
ribbons!"

"I'm not your grandson, not
at all," screamed Tojiro. "Me,
I'm going to sell rice cakes

54

at the Kabuki theater. I'll be a great actor, and also the fiercest sumo wrestler of all time!"

"Very well, in that case give me my paintbrushes back, little scamp," thundered the old man.

"No," screamed Tojiro. "Never!"

And suddenly he awoke with the first rays of the sun.

His eyes still puffy with sleep, the young boy washed up in the garden, bowed to his uncle and his aunt, quickly ate breakfast, and ran to the old painter's. At the garden gate, Hokusai greeted him with his usual sly smile.

"Well, well, our young sparrow doesn't seem quite himself today. Did he fall out of his nest?"

Tojiro sulkily entered without answering.

The painter didn't take offense. He sent the boy to the well for water so he could prepare his ink. Tojiro came back carrying a bucket with twigs and dust floating on top.

"Come now, sparrow! What can I do with water like that? It's not water, it's mud. In fact it's a little like you; it's scowling at me."

"But it's to make ink," the child protested. "It will be even blacker than it is in the bucket!"

"Don't argue. Use this cotton cloth to filter the water and fill this little teapot. I want water that is *limpid*."

"Okay, okay," the child grumbled.

When Tojiro came back, the painter carefully poured the pure water into a suzuri. This is an inkstone, a shallow rectangular container whose slanted bottom forms the reservoir. Then he took a stick of ink and rubbed it on the abrasive bottom. Slowly, the water took on a beautiful dark black color.

"Look at how beautiful this ink is. Now do you under-stand why I needed clear water? Water is the brightness of day and the whiteness of paper. Black is the velvet of night and the satiny ink of the paintbrush. If you know how to make ink correctly, you will never again be afraid of nightmares."

"Hmph! I never have nightmares!"

"Believe me, little sparrow, he who knows how to tame the white of paper and the black of the night can draw all of his dreams and his nightmares."

"Is that true?" asked Tojiro.

"That's what I've been doing ever since I was your age."

THE MASTER'S
THIRTY-SIX BIRTHS

In the weeks that followed, Tojiro made rapid progress. He learned how to make ink according to the master's needs, to clean the suzuri and the brushes, to prepare and cut paper. He worked at calligraphy, learned to read, brought the master's sketches to the engraving studio, and above all, enchanted the old man with his carefree gaiety.

As a reward at the end of each morning, the boy immersed himself in one of the painter's many books.

"Master," he asked one day, "didn't you tell me that you illustrated this book?"

"Yes, sparrow, but don't bother me. I'm working on a difficult drawing."

"Master, and this one: did you illustrate it also?"

"Yes, that was me," the old painter said with a sigh. "Leave me alone. I'm working."

"But why didn't you sign them with the same name?"

"You know, if I had to add up all the names that I have signed, it would take all morning and I wouldn't have gotten anything done. An artist like me changes names every time he starts a new period of his life or changes his way of painting and drawing.

"For example, I changed names when I left the studio of Katsukawa Shunsho, my first master. I was beginning to be well known for my pictures of Kabuki actors, and had painted a very beautiful poster for a neighborhood print seller. One of my workmates, passing before this merchant's store, noticed it and tore it up. He thought that it didn't match our studio's style.

"I mainly think he was jealous, because it was really

a magnificent piece of work. But because he was more senior than me – there was nothing I could say. So I got angry and left the studio. At that time I was signing my name as Shunro, and I changed it to Sori. Then I signed it Hokusai, which means 'North Star studio,' and I decided to follow my own path, that of 'a free spirit soaring above the summer plains.' Each new period of my life was like a new birth, which is why I used so many signatures. Of course you know what name I sign today, sparrow: Gakyo-rojin Hokusai, 'Old Man Mad About Drawing.' What do you think of it?"

"That one suits you perfectly!" said Tojiro, bursting into laughter.

"You shouldn't make fun of me. Do you know that I was once visited by the shogun in person with his entire guard, when he was coming back from hawking?"

"You? The shogun and his samurai guard?"

At the thought, Tojiro's eyes opened wide.

"That's right, sparrow. The samurai, the courtesans, and the shogun, all mounted on their splendid horses, wearing their hunting clothes and carrying the best-trained hawks in the country on their gloved fists."

"But how?"

"Thanks to my reputation as a painter, of course. I didn't just illustrate cheap little books; I was a well-known artist. I visited the poetry clubs: the Drunken Bamboo Club, the Flowered Hat Club, and the Disheveled Chrysanthemums Club. I could tell you many things about that. It was a joyful, witty, and cultivated world. And I collaborated with many writers, like Bakin."

"Bakin?"

"Yes, Bakin. You'll like him. He's the son of a samurai. He wrote dozens of novels about the extraordinary adventures of Chinese and Japanese warriors. They were very popular among the samurai and the shogun and his court, as a matter of fact.

"But listen to my story. It was a day in autumn, I remember it very well. I was painting, with the screen open to the garden, when I saw a large group of riders stop in front of my house.

"The shogun had himself announced, and asked in a friendly way if I would paint something for him. He wanted to see me at work, he said, because my reputation had reached beyond the walls of his palace.

"I immediately ordered my helper to spread a large roll of paper on the floor and to put a pot of light ink in front of me. Using a broad brush, I very quickly set about drawing the waves of a river. Up to then the noblemen had watched me at work in respectful silence, but I sensed a slight agitation among them when I asked my apprentice to bring me a rooster."

"A rooster?"

"A rooster, yes. I dipped the rooster's feet in purple ink and made it walk on the drawing."

"Oh..."

"Each of its footprints was exactly the shape of a tree leaf. . . . All I had to do was sign my name. As a last step, I wrote a short poem above my drawing: 'Red Leaves on the Tatsuta River.' The shogun and his company greatly admired the drawing."

"And what if the rooster had walked off the paper? The shogun would have thought you were making fun of him."

"That was a risk to be taken, and it amused me. Sometimes the shogun forbade certain books or prints. Some of my friends had even been forced to stop publishing, and others went to prison. But we loved liberty too much not to have fun at the expense of censorship or the shogun's

63

ill temper. Well, I have to get back to work. I'm going to lend you this book by Bakin. Try and get somebody to help you read it. When you're finished, I'll give you another one with the sequel."

"The sequel?"

"Yes, the sequel. Beware – it's a story in twenty volumes."

"So much the better! I love stories about warriors!"

C
H
A
P
T
E
R
10

The more time passed, the more pleasure Tojiro took in his morning meetings with the old painter. His curiosity grew as well, and he never tired of exploring the library. He could not have imagined there were so many topics for books: stories, satirical books, collections of poetry, descriptions of the city of Edo, novels, stories about ghosts and spirits, and treatises on natural history. They were due to the old painter's magic. From one page to the next, he could bring the most extraordinary things and beings to life with a few brushstrokes: tengu with pointed noses, mice dressed like townspeople, a valiant warrior doing battle with a giant spider.

The old painter claimed he had written many

一物巧機多
綾羅一不用祓
一身供一口
無奈一身何

of these works himself, but how could you be sure, with all the signatures he used?

One fine day Tojiro began to laugh and do dance steps around the studio. The master looked up from his drawing.

"Hey, sparrow, what's gotten into you?"

"Look what I found, master," he said, holding up a little book called *Teach Yourself to Dance*.

"Aha! I remember that one," chuckled the master. "I had dreamed of dancing all night long and, if you can believe it, at dawn I woke up thinking I knew how to dance!

"I immediately took paper and a brush and I began to draw all the dances I could think of: the boatman's dance, the water seller's dance, the evil-spirit dance, and so forth. Naturally, all of this was more or less made up. I'm even sure that anyone who tried to dance by following the steps I drew had every chance of immediately landing on his behind on the ground!"

"Ha, ha, ha!" Tojiro wept with laughter imagining the old painter executing clownish figures in his studio.

And suddenly he was hopping all around the room, imitating his grumpy-looking master.

"Hee, hee, hee! An old man like you, as stiff as a

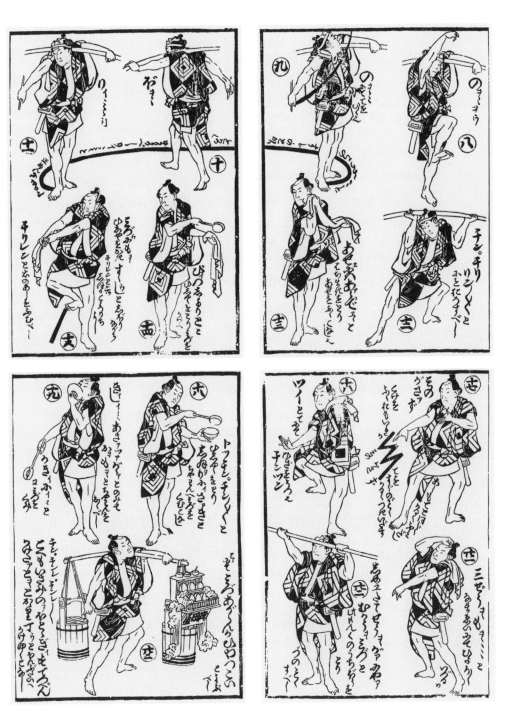

chimney tile, dancing with wooden clogs! I can't believe it! I just can't believe it!"

"Hey, enough of that, sparrow! I didn't take you in so you could make fun of me! Are you provoking me? Very well, *en garde!* Defend yourself! We'll see if you have what it takes to make a samurai."

As if possessed by the demon of the dance, the old painter and Tojiro began to circle each other, each threatening the other with the tip of a paintbrush. An attack was launched: hop! A quick step to the side. Entrechats, grimaces, parries, offensives – they didn't miss a trick.

The old man gave hoarse, half-strangled roars and glowered beneath his bushy eyebrows. The boy rolled his eyes while hopping this way and that.

It all ended in an attack of laughter that shook them for long minutes.

"Thank you, sparrow," said the master when they finally calmed down. "That reminded me of my duels with my friend Bakin. We've argued with each other so many times! And we've laughed many more times than that! You're on the right path. A good artist should laugh often!"

C
H
A
P
T
E
R

11

I'm going to take you for a walk today, sparrow. The weather is too nice to stay in the studio, and anyway, I feel like walking."

They set off through the narrow streets where everything was so familiar, and they could recognize every workshop's noises, smells, and cries. Determined to show how much he knew, Tojiro thrust out his little sparrow chest and was chattering nonstop when Hokusai suddenly stopped him and gestured for him to be quiet.

"Shhhh . . . look," he said, pointing. "Look at the butterfly on the peony."

Both of them froze, and there was as much wonder in the old man's eyes as in the child's. When they started walking together again, the master took Tojiro's hand and whispered in his ear: "Learn to look in silence, if you don't want noise to drive away the beauty of fragile things that are before your eyes."

As they made their way along, they passed beneath a torii, a large stone gateway at the entrance of a Shinto shrine.

"Master," Tojiro suddenly said, "I'd like to make a wish and pray to the fox god."

"Well, in that case let's go in," suggested the old man.

They washed their hands in the water of a spring, and in the first courtyard bowed before a large censer, gently breathing the fragrant incense smoke rising in the cool morning air. Tall trees created a welcome shade, and a small stream sang as it cascaded between moss-covered rocks. A row of stone lanterns led to a pavilion that sheltered a heavy bronze bell. A Shinto priest, accompanied by two acolytes, was ringing it to bring the good-will of the gods to the shrine.

Tojiro bowed before an

altar consecrated to the fox god. In his heart of hearts he asked the god to give him the same talent as his master. Smiling, the old man watched as the child prayed.

"Master," asked Tojiro as he straightened up, "aren't you going to pray with me to the fox god?"

"No, sparrow. I'm a Buddhist. Some other day, I'll take you with me to the temple of Daruma, if you like. The monk who looks after that temple is a friend of mine, and I would like to give him a painting to thank Daruma for giving me such a long life."

"It's true that you're old," Tojiro remarked seriously, "but I find you younger than my uncle. How old would you like to live?"

"I hope until a hundred, sparrow, and longer if I can. . . ."

THE CHALLENGE

I'm hungry," said the old painter as they left the shrine. "Would you like me to buy you something to nibble on, sparrow?"

The two sat down at an open-air stall. Hokusai ordered soba – delicious buckwheat noodles – and norimaki, balls of rice and vegetables wrapped in dried seaweed, and a pot of green tea for himself.

"Have you ever heard about the huge portrait of Daruma I once painted?"

"No," answered the boy, who was stuffing himself as fast as he could eat.

"No?" said the painter, a little

disappointed. "It's a well-known story, and I'm surprised that a boy of your age doesn't know it. It's true that it happened at Nagoya."

"Nagoya? Never heard of it!"

"Well," said the old man with some annoyance, "I hope you'll make use of your wings to fly away some day, sparrow. There are other cities than the one where you were born. Who knows? Maybe one day you'll pick up your pilgrim's staff and take to the Tokaido Road, which leads to Kyoto, our venerable imperial city.

"It's a wonderful road, believe me. You meet all sorts of people on it: merchants, pilgrims, and traveling ladies from the court, with the snows of Mount Fuji high above everything. Yes indeed, I could well imagine your little face as you walk along that high road with your things in a bundle . . . but where was I?"

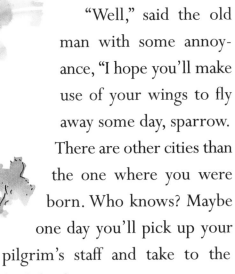

"At Nagoya, master."

"That's right, Nagoya. . . . Let's see, it was the year 1817. . . . Heh-heh! You hadn't climbed out of the nest yet, sparrow. I was staying with friends there, and in that city there were people who were jealous of me. They claimed I wasn't a real artist, supposedly because I illustrated too many 'popular' books."

"But I think your books are very beautiful."

"Ah, don't interrupt me, please! So people were saying, 'That Hokusai, he's gifted, he clearly knows his craft, but he doesn't have the slightest genius! He's not nearly as good as Utamaro! He's just a common artist!' A common artist! Do you hear? It's as if they had never seen any of my paintings. Can you imagine, sparrow?"

The old painter was so angry he spilled his tea.

Tojiro raised his eyes from his bowl and glanced at his master. More than ever, Hokusai looked like an old madman, with the tufts of white hair on his ancient skull standing straight up and flames seeming to dart from his eyes.

"My friends got together to defend me, and they suggested that I demonstrate my talent in a really striking way. We decided that I would paint a huge portrait of Daruma in the courtyard of the great Nagoya temple. We

had posters put up all over town to announce the event:
'On the fifth day of the tenth month of the Year of the Ox,

Hokusai Taito Gakyojin, our guest from the Eastern Capital, will create a giant portrait of Daruma!' And believe me, plenty of people read them!"

The old painter's face became more and more animated. He put all the conviction and fire of his youth into his words, to the point where Tojiro thought he was seeing a kind of demon of drawing and painting before him, shaken by a violent rage. Forgetting to eat, the boy sat with his chin in his hands, ears wide open to the old painter's story.

CHAPTER 13

The dawn of the great day finally arrived. Preparations had been underway for more than two weeks, and my assistants had worked through the night. In the temple courtyard, a huge sheet of paper had been laid out on a rice-straw mat specially woven for the occasion. Strips of wood set at regular intervals kept the wind from lifting the enormous sheet.

"I had some huge brushes made out of rice straw and bamboo. Great quantities of ink in wooden buckets were set out all around the gigantic white sheet.

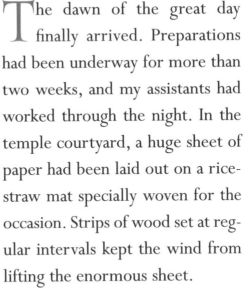

"All of the town notables were sitting in a grandstand, and the crowd gathered in the temple courtyard behind barriers guarded by the monks.

"I entered at daybreak, wearing wide ceremonial pants and a tunic with the sleeves tied up, followed by my oldest students. I started by drawing the curve of Daruma's eye. As this huge eye appeared on the paper, gazing at the sky, five thousand pairs of eyes were riveted earthward, watching me at work. An assistant handed me a second brush, and I drew the eyebrow. Then I had to take several steps so I could start the curve of a second eye. Imagine, Tojiro: the painter walking across his work as he creates it!

"By the end of the morning, Daruma's face was finished. I then took a brush that was even wider than the previous ones and, dragging it with a rope over my shoulder, I started drawing the robe.

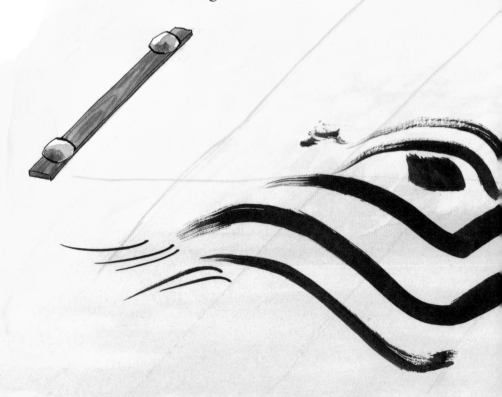

"It looked like the sides of a mountain, on which this strange pairing – the brush and I – was walking, while I gave it shape.

"When the drawing was finished, I had my assistants throw buckets of paint on it while others soaked up the excess with wet cloths.

"By the end of the afternoon, the portrait was finished.

"All that was left was to hoist it onto its scaffolding.

"At my signal, several teams of muscular men started to pull on the heavy ropes that ran through the pulleys of the crossbar on which the drawing was to be hung.

"I'm sure you would have enjoyed shouting, 'Heave ho! Heave ho!' along with the crowd, as the portrait slowly rose above it. As it turned out, it was so big that it couldn't be raised all the way.

"Everyone then crowded around to admire it, as eager as an army of ants around a piece of cake!

"And that, my dear sparrow, is how the inhabitants of Nagoya came to know me as 'Daruma Sensei,' or 'Daruma's Master!'"

CHAPTER 14

THE GREAT WAVE

Snow blanketed the great city. It was cold. Everywhere, people were digging out the roads and pathways. Tojiro had been coming to the old painter's studio every morning for ten months. The room was heated by a brazier, and the master set his table close to it, so the ink on his brushes wouldn't freeze. Not a day went by without him working.

Sometimes he would grow angry; on other days he had a kind of smile in his eyes. Today, joy blossomed in his look. The first drawing of the morning had put him in a good mood. It showed a shishi rolling in the snow.

Tojiro had finished his writing exercises. Bundled up in a corner

85

of the studio, the child was looking at the prints of *Thirty-Six Views of Mount Fuji*, a collection that came out in 1830. Among all of the images, one fascinated him especially. It was called *The Great Wave at Kanagawa*.

It showed a monstrous wave about to break over some fishermen's boats, while in the distance you could see the tiny snowy cone of Mount Fuji.

How had the master gone about stopping time in this way? The wave seemed alive, boiling with foam, and you could see it ready to come crashing down. By the mere magic of his drawing, the master had fixed for eternity the two most fluid elements in the universe: water and time.

Tojiro then looked up and shot a look of gratitude toward the old painter, who was still bent over his work.

LEARNING TO DRAW

CHAPTER 15

Friends of the master, painters and men of letters, sometimes came to visit. They would drink tea and talk at length about the qualities and merits of various people, or of the reputation of this or that fashionable painter. But to Tojiro it was obvious that his master still dominated the conversations on those occasions with the accuracy of his criticisms and the soundness of his judgment, revealing his prodigious literary and artistic culture.

"When do you plan to teach this boy to draw, dear Hokusai? His eyes are already burning with the same fire as yours."

Tojiro pricked up his ears. Were they talking about him? He had never dared to ask the master for a drawing lesson before. The old man paid attention mainly to his progress in writing and read-

89

ing, and for the rest, advised him to open his eyes and to look carefully at the books that he loaned him.

"I could give him books to learn to draw, *Quick-Draw Guide to Drawing*, or *One-Brushstroke Drawings*, but the sparrow still seems a little young. He has barely left the nest and still doesn't hold a brush properly."

In spite of himself Tojiro felt tears coming to his eyes. "The master is just selfish," he thought. "He's very old, he knows a great deal, and he doesn't want to share it."

When his friends finally left, the old painter came to sit near Tojiro, who was still feeling very disappointed and sad.

Hokusai set a box on the tatami mat and took ten small books out of it.

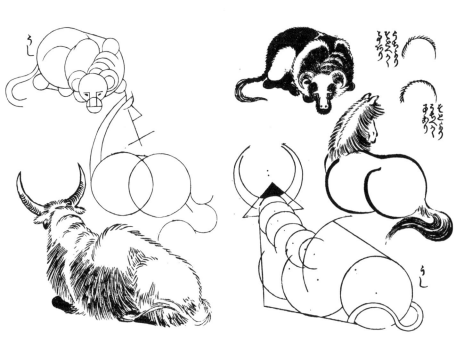

"You know, sparrow, this isn't the first time that I've been asked to teach others to draw. I even thought of creating books for that: a manual for drawing with a single brushstroke, and another that would teach people to use the circle and the square, the two primary shapes for creating a drawing. But my friends were never satisfied. One day, one of them even suggested that I didn't really want to transmit what I knew, which is the worst of insults for a man like me, believe me. Several of us were talking and the conversation was beginning to turn nasty. To cut the criticism short, I suddenly stood up and said: 'So you want to learn to draw? Very well, watch me – and learn, if you like!'

"I took a great bundle of sheets of paper, ink, and a brush, and began to draw everything that came to my mind, as quick as thought, without stopping.

"A mountain? Here it is. A bunch of beggars? Here they are. Acrobats, a cascade, a pine forest, three frogs, a stick fight, a woman combing her hair, an old man yawning, a dog in the snow, a cricket, a peasant in the rain? They all came to life right there under my rapid brushstrokes. I barely raised my hand except to put more ink in my brush. This was in Nagoya, in Gekkotei Bokusen's house. . . .

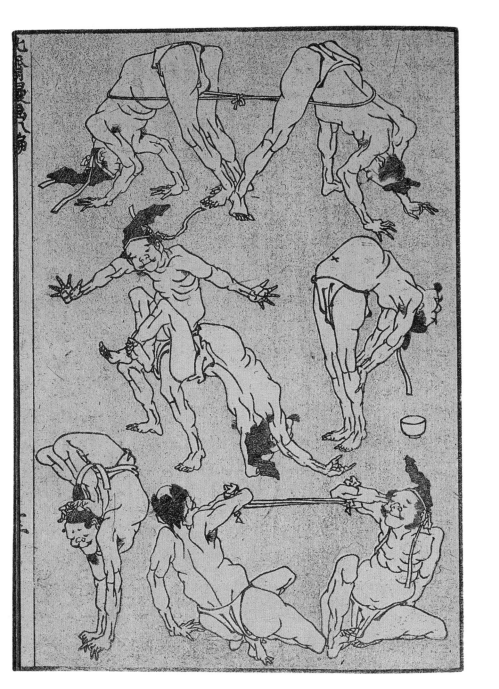

"I drew all day long. Caught up in the game, my friends suggested things for me to draw.

"Later, a publisher friend wanted to reproduce these drawings in an album. The idea appealed to me, so I drew hundreds more, enough for several books. I called them manga, 'thought-up drawings,' and these collections became known as the *Hokusai Manga*.

"Look at them, Tojiro. They are the fruit of an entire life of observation. As I've grown older I've become more and more interested in the variety of the shapes in nature. What you have before your eyes is a true encyclopedia in drawings. When you have studied them carefully you will already know a great deal; but you will learn the essential with your hand, your eyes, and your heart."

95

When the young boy had feasted his eyes, the old painter continued the conversation.

"By the way, sparrow, if you really want to learn to draw, you will need real tools." In front of the boy he set a booklet of bound white sheets, and an odd lacquer case shaped like a pipe.

"Always keep this yatate on your belt. And never hesitate to use it wherever you may be, at any time, on any occasion. For those of us who like to draw, this is our sword."

Tojiro opened the case's cover. Inside was a tiny inkwell, and in the sleeve, a brand-new brush.

THE OLD MAN MAD
ABOUT DRAWING

On May 5, Boys' Day, Tojiro's uncle invited the old painter to spend the day with his family. It was actually just about the only time when the rice-cake seller showed himself to be proud of his adopted son. Like all of Edo's inhabitants, he had decorated his house with a paper carp that danced in the wind, symbolizing the child's vitality.

The entire neighborhood was celebrating, and people were drinking and eating more than usual — or reasonable. Tojiro's uncle, under the effect of the jugs of sake that

his wife kept refilling, hugged the old painter in a familiar way and praised him for getting his worthless nephew to learn so much.

Hokusai laughed cheerfully, Tojiro ate rice cakes until he was ready to burst, and the party lasted long after nightfall in the dancing light of paper lanterns. Finally, after a last cup, the old painter spoke to his student.

His voice suddenly became serious, and the family listened to him in silence.

"You have grown a lot, Tojiro, and your uncle can be proud of you. With his consent I have written to one of my friends, a master engraver in Nagasaki. He is prepared to take you in his service and teach you the trade. This is a wonderful opportunity for you. You will finally be able to travel! There is a trading post for European merchants there. They have different customs and know other techniques. A young boy like you should be open to different worlds. But don't make too much fun of their long noses; they're quite touchy.

"Follow your new master's advice carefully. Carving wood blocks will teach you discipline, which is a good thing to learn. That way, when you pick up your brush, you'll do it with a firm, sure hand. If you want to think of me, draw a shishi every morning. And above all, write me when you feel like it. I will never fail to answer you."

Tojiro nodded his head. He didn't want to cry on Boys' Day, but in spite of himself, his eyes filled with tears.

Hokusai slipped a package wrapped in cotton in front of him.

"Open it, Tojiro. It's a present."

Swallowing his tears, Tojiro opened the cloth, revealing the old painter's gift: the first ten books of the *Manga*!

The morning after that strange day, Tojiro came to say goodbye to the master. On the table where the young boy liked to read, the old painter had laid his famous album, *One Hundred Views of Mount Fuji*. Tojiro leafed sadly through it. Suddenly, he came to the last page where the following words were written:

From the age of six I started drawing all sorts of things. At fifty I had already drawn a great deal, but nothing that I did before my seventieth year was worth any great note. It was at seventy-three that I began to understand the true shape of animals, insects, and fishes, and the nature of plants and trees.

Therefore, at eighty-six I will have made more and more progress, and at ninety I shall have penetrated even further into the essence of art. At a hundred I will certainly have reached a marvelous stage, and at a hundred and ten each dot and line of my drawings will have a life of its own. I would like to ask those who survive me to ascertain whether I have not spoken without reason.

Hokusai, Old Man Mad About Drawing.

Tojiro then turned toward the old painter and told him:

"I will learn!"

GLOSSARY

*The Japanese painter Hokusai lived from 1760
to 1849, in the Edo Period. At that time, Japan
had two capitals: Kyoto, the imperial city where
the emperor lived, and Edo, the "Eastern Capital," which was the seat of the government
headed by the shogun, who was both prime min-
ister and commander in chief.*

BONZE

A monk or priest in the Buddhist religion.

BOYS' DAY

For Boys' Day, which takes place on the
fifth day of the fifth month, people hang
cloth or paper carps on bamboo poles
above their houses.

BUDDHISM

Buddhism, a religion of Indian origin that
embodies Buddha's precepts and teach-
ings, was introduced to Japan in the sixth
century.

CALLIGRAPHY

The Japanese very early adopted Chinese
writing, which uses a very large number of
ideograms, and they also invented their
own characters. Calligraphy, which
is done with a brush and ink,
is a distinct art form.

DARUMA

A fifth-century Indian sage and the first patriarch of Zen Buddhism. He is also known as Daruma Daishi in Japan, and is represented by a popular doll called a "Daruma." The doll is used as a charm to fulfill some special wish, such as success on an examination or election to public office. It is customary to paint one eye in black when the wish is made, then paint the second eye after the wish is fulfilled.

FOX GOD

The fox, the messenger of Inari, god of rice paddies, is much loved by children.

GEISHA

In the pleasure quarter's teahouses, geishas are women who practice the arts of singing, music, and dance.

GIRLS' DAY

For Girls' Day, which is celebrated on the third day of the third month, dolls in court dress are displayed on stands in the house's living room.

KABUKI

A theatrical form with a repertoire that is known and enjoyed by the public. All of the actors are men, even those who take female roles.

MOUNT FUJI

This volcano, with its almost perfect conical shape, is Japan's sacred mountain. It appears in a very large number of paintings and prints.

NAGASAKI

An island off the coast of Nagasaki that was occupied by Dutch merchants. It was the only trading post where commerce with Europeans was allowed.

RONIN

A ronin was a samurai who no longer served a lord. In the feudal era, ronin were often bandits.

SAKE

Rice wine, drunk hot or cold.

SAMURAI

Samurai were warriors who traditionally served a lord. They always carried two swords, but wore armor only when going into battle.

SHINTO

This religion consists of beliefs and practices that are special to Japan. It honors the emperor as well as a large number of divinities and spirits, the kami. Its magnificent shrines are built in parks or gardens that exalt the feeling of nature.

SHOGUN

In the Edo Period, there was an emperor and a shogun. The shogun was the commander of all the armies and the head of government, and the real ruler of Japan. His castle overlooked the city of Edo.

SUZURI

An inkstone, or suzuri, is a shallow stone container with an abrasive, slanted bottom. You put a little water into it, then rub the ink stick on the bottom. This is the way ink was traditionally made in both China and Japan.

TATAMI

A thick, very dense rice-straw mat used to cover the floor in some houses. A single tatami is about the size of a small mattress.

TENGU

In Japanese stories and legends, this is a goblin or devil that has bird's wings, a long nose, or a bird's head.

TOKAIDO

The road connecting Edo to Kyoto, the shogun's capital to the emperor's. Many prints show its most notable landscapes and famous stages: the bridges, fords, inns, and temples, where merchants, pilgrims, and ordinary "tourists" would meet.

TORII

A large stone or wooden gateway that marks a sacred place, often the entrance of a shrine or temple, but also certain natural sites, such as rocks and beaches.

YATATE

A little writing kit that consists of an inkwell and a tube to store a brush.

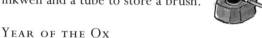

YEAR OF THE OX

The ancient Japanese calendar was like the Chinese one, where each year in the twelve-year cycle is represented by an animal.

Page 19: Shishi (lion-dragon), drawing from the series *Nisshin Joma (Daily Exorcisms)*, 1842–1843. Page 24–25: Arikinu killing Sunosuke, an illustration for the novel *Bei-Bei Kyodan (A Rustic Tale of Two Heirs)*, 1815. Page 37: Woman in court dress, with a fan at her feet. A surimono from the series *Gosaken (The Five Women Poets)*, circa. 1823. Dublin, the Chester Beatty Library. Page 43: The actor Ichikawa Ebizo IV in the role of Mongaku, disguised as a woodcutter. London, The British Museum. The actor Sakata Hongoro III in the role of Chinzei Hachiro Tametomo, disguised as a wandering monk. Diptych print, 1791. Boston, The Museum of Fine Arts. Photo © MFA, Boston. Page 66–67: Sonobaesemon Yoritane and the giant spider, an illustration for the novel *Sono no yuki (The Snow of the Garden)*, 1807. Leyden, Rijksmuseum voor Volkenkunde. Photo © Ben Grishaaver. Page 69: The water-seller's dance, illustration from the album *Odori hitori keiko (Teach Yourself to Dance)*. Leyden, Rijksmuseum voor Volkenkunde. Photo © Ben Grishaaver. Page 86–87: The Great Wave at Kanagawa, a print from the series *Fugaku sanjurokkei (Thirty-Six Views of Mount Fuji)*, circa 1830. London, The British Museum. Photo © The British Museum. Page 91: How to draw an ox and a horse, illustration from the album *Ryakuga hayashinan (Quick-Draw Guide to Drawing)*, vol. 1, 1812. Paris, private collection. Photo © Patrick Léger, Gallimard Jeunesse. Sparrows, illustration from *Ippitsu gafu (One-Brushstroke Drawings)*, circa 1816, published in 1824. Leyden, Rijksmuseum voor Volkenkunde. Photo © Ben Grishaaver. Page 93: Acrobats, illustration from the album *Hokusai manga (The Hokusai Sketchbooks)*, vol. 8, circa 1819. London, The British Museum. Photo © Bridgeman-Giraudon. Page 94–94: Scenes of daily life, illustrations from the album *Hokusai manga (The Hokusai Sketchbooks)*, vol. 8, circa 1819. Dublin, the Chester Beatty Library. Photo © Ben Grishaaver.

A NOTE ON THE TYPE

The Old Man Mad About Drawing has been set in a digital version of Monotype Perpetua. Designed by Eric Gill after the style of his inscriptional lettering, the original foundry type was cut by the renowned French punchcutter Charles Malin. The type made its first appearance, in the 1 3 -point size, in a private printing of Walter Shewring's translation of *The Passion of Perpetua and Felicity* in 1 9 2 8. The italic, originally christened 'Felicity,' appeared shortly thereafter. Both faces were made available for machine composition on the Monotype in 1 9 2 9. Perpetua's success lies in its distinctive letterforms, which give the impression that they were cut with a burin, rather than drawn with a pen. As Stanley Morison commented in his *Tally of Types*, "Perpetua is a design appropriate for select classes of work with which a certain obvious 'style' is desired. . . . Perpetua may be judged in the small sizes to have achieved the object of providing a distinguished form for a distinguished text; and, in the large sizes, a noble monumental, appearance."

Design and composition by
Carl W. Scarbrough